THE BIGGEST, BEST SNOWMAN

BY **MARGERY CUYLER**

ILLUSTRATED BY **WILL HILLENBRAND**

SCHOLASTIC INC.

New York Toronto London Auckland Sydney
Mexico City New Delhi Hong Kong Buenos Aires

This book was originally published in hardcover by Scholastic Press in 1998.

ISBN-13: 978-0-439-66940-5
ISBN-10: 0-439-66940-5
Text copyright © 1998 by Margery Cuyler
Illustrations copyright © 1998 by Will Hillenbrand
All rights reserved. Published by Scholastic Inc.
SCHOLASTIC, SCHOLASTIC PRESS, and associated logos are trademarks and/or registered trademarks of Scholastic Inc.

12 11 10 9 8 7 6   8 9 10 11 12/0

Printed in the U.S.A.   40
First Bookshelf edition, October 2004
Design by Will Hillenbrand and Becky Terhune

For Will Hillenbrand, with thanks for the Christmas card that inspired this story, and for Carol Vukelich. — M. C.

For Ian my son, Jane my wife, and a BIG November snow, my inspiration. — W. H.

Little Nell lived with BIG Mama, BIG Sarah, and BIG Lizzie in a BIG house in a BIG snowy woods.

BIG Mama, BIG Sarah, and BIG Lizzie
had BIG blustery voices. They had
BIG talky friends. They had BIG loud parties.
   When Little Nell asked, "Can I help?"
BIG Mama, BIG Sarah, and BIG Lizzie shook
their heads. "No, you can't," they said.
"You're too small."

"Yes, I can," said Little Nell,
"and no, I'm not."
"No, you can't," they said,
"and yes, you are!"

So Little Nell would go into the BIG snowy
woods. She would sit and watch the snow
fall from the sky. She would walk under the
bare-branched trees. She would play with
her friends, Reindeer, Hare, and Bear Cub.

One day, Bear Cub said to Little Nell, "Can you show us how to make a snowman?"

"No, I can't," said Little Nell. "I'm too small."

"Yes, you can," said the animals, "and no, you're not!"

"But I'm so small," said Little Nell, "my family won't let me do anything. I could never make a snowman."

"How do you know unless you try?" asked Bear Cub. "We'll help you."

Little Nell sighed. "Well, maybe," she said.

Little Nell got down on her knees.
She carefully patted and matted and
batted the snow into a tiny ball.

She rolled it and rolled it and rolled
it to Reindeer. Reindeer nudged it and
nudged it and nudged it to Hare.

Hare kicked it and kicked it and
kicked it to Bear Cub.

Bear Cub rolled it and rolled it
and rolled it until it stopped — THUD —
by the edge of a BIG icy pond.

"Now what?" asked Reindeer.

"The snowman needs a middle," said Little Nell.

"How do we do that?" asked Hare.

Little Nell bit her lip. She got down on her knees. She carefully patted and matted and batted another tiny snowball.

She rolled it and rolled it to Reindeer. Reindeer nudged it and nudged it to Hare. Hare kicked it and kicked it to Bear Cub.

Bear Cub rolled it and rolled it
until — THUD — it came to a stop.
He pushed it on top of the other
snowball.

"Now what?" he asked.

"It needs a head!" cried Little Nell.
She patted and matted and batted
another tiny snowball. Then she
rolled it to Reindeer. Reindeer nudged
it to Hare. Hare kicked it to Bear Cub.

Bear Cub stuck it on top
of the other two snowballs.

Little Nell and the animals stood back and looked at their snowman.

"Something's missing," said Hare.

"The face," said Little Nell.

"How do we do that?" asked the animals.

"I think we'll need help," said Little Nell.

She whistled for the birds to come. Crow, Cardinal, and Sparrow flew down from the trees.

"Could you make a face for our snowman?" she asked.

Crow fetched two pieces of bark for the eyes.

Cardinal found an old pink sock for the nose.

Sparrow brought raisins for the mouth.

Little Nell handed her green scarf to the birds. They wound it and wound it and wound it around the snowman's neck. Then they added two sticks for arms.

The snowman was finally finished.

Little Nell and the animals gazed up at their creation.

"Wow!" said the animals.

"Wow!" said Little Nell.

It was almost lunchtime. Little
Nell said good-bye to her friends.
She walked home through the
BIG snowy woods.

BIG Mama, BIG Sarah, and BIG Lizzie were waiting for her.
"Where have you been?" they asked in their BIG blustery voices.
"I was building a great big snowman," answered Little Nell.
"How could someone as little as you build a great BIG snowman?" asked BIG Lizzie.
"Come and see," said Little Nell.

So BIG Mama, BIG Sarah, and BIG
Lizzie followed Little Nell through the
BIG snowy woods to the snowman.

As they looked up, their mouths dropped open and their arms dropped to their sides.

"Wow!" they said. "You built that?"

"Yes, I did," said Little Nell, "with the help of my friends."

"That is the biggest, best snowman that ever was," said BIG Mama.

"Yes, it is," said Little Nell, a huge smile on her face.

"Will you come and help us make a BIG yummy lunch?" asked BIG Sarah.

"No, she can't," said BIG Lizzie. "She's still too small."

"Yes, I can," said Little Nell, "and no, I'm not!"

"Yes, you can," said BIG Mama, "and yes, you WILL!"

BIG Mama gave Little Nell a BIG sloppy kiss — SMOOCH!
BIG Sarah gave Little Nell a BIG squeezy hug — OOCH!
BIG Lizzie stuck her BIG nose in the air — HMMPH!

Little Nell's friends lifted her
to the top of the snowman —